Hurricanes

BY CHRISTY STEELE

Steadwell
Books

Raintree Steck-Vaughn Publishers
A Harcourt Company

Austin · New York
www.steck-vaughn.com

Nature
on the
Rampage

Published by Raintree Steck-Vaughn Publishers,
an imprint of Steck-Vaughn Company.
Library of Congress Cataloging-in-Publication Data
Steele, Christy.
    Hurricanes/by Christy Steele.
        p.cm.--(Nature on the rampage)
    Includes index.
    Summary: Explains how hurricanes start and what effects they
have on the environment.
    ISBN 0-7398-1793-0
    1. Hurricanes--Juvenile literature. [1. Hurricanes.] I. Title. II.
Series.
QC944.2 .S74 2000
551.55'2--dc21

                                                               99-059092

Printed in the United States of America
10 9 8 7 6 5 4 3 2 1 LB 02 01 00

Produced by Compass Books

Photo Acknowledgments
Archive Photos/Reuters/Ana Martinez, cover, 4;
Reuters/Rick Wilking, 16
Digital Stock, 10, 20, 22, 24, 27, 29
Photo Network/Jeff Greenberg, 18
Photophile, 12

Content Consultant
Frank Lepore
National Hurricane Center

CONTENTS

HOW HURRICANES START

Hurricanes are some of nature's strongest storms. Hurricanes are made up of bands of thunderstorms. Powerful winds and Earth's spinning movement make the bands of thunderstorms rotate. Rotate means to circle. The thunderstorms rotate around the center of the storm.

Hurricanes are large storms. They may be 10 miles (16 km) high. They can be 1,000 miles (1,609 km) wide.

Hurricanes can blow down trees and houses. Rain from hurricanes can cause floods.

 Hurricane winds can blow down trees.

Naming Hurricanes

Scientists came up with a way to name hurricanes in 1978. Scientists pick a name for each letter of the alphabet except Q, U, X, Y, and Z. Not many names start with these letters. Each new storm gets a name beginning with the next letter of the alphabet.

Some hurricane names are used only once. A hurricane's name is not used again if the storm causes much death and property loss. Andrew, Camille, Carmen, Donna, Bob, Mitch, and Gilbert were killer hurricanes. Their names will never be used again.

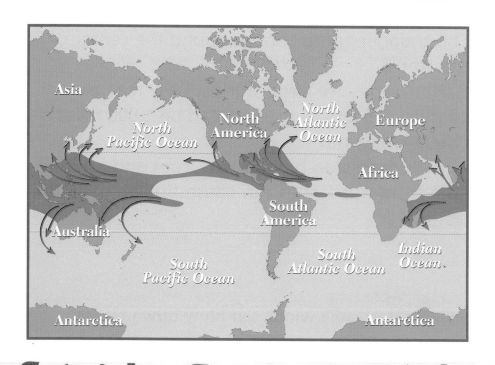

Where and When Hurricanes Form

Hurricanes start over warm, tropical water near the equator. The equator is an imaginary line around the center of Earth. It divides Earth into two equal parts. Tropical areas where many hurricanes begin are called hurricane basins. Many hurricanes that hit North America start in a basin near Africa.

Hurricane season lasts from May or June through November. But hurricanes can happen during any month of the year. Most hurricanes start during mid-August through October. Ocean water is warmer during late summer to early fall. The sun has heated the water all summer.

A hurricane's strength depends on how warm the water is. The warmer the water gets, the stronger the hurricane will be.

 This map shows where many hurricanes begin.

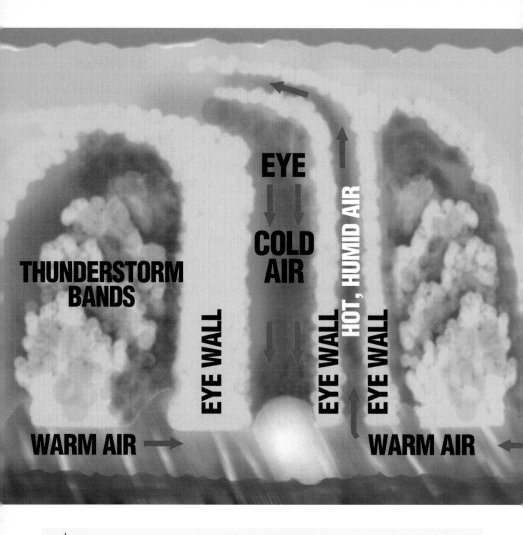

EYE

COLD
AIR

THUNDERSTORM
BANDS

EYE WALL

EYE WALL

HOT, HUMID AIR

EYE WALL

WARM AIR →

WARM AIR ←

▲ This diagram shows the parts of a hurricane.

A Hurricane Starts

Hurricanes start over warm ocean water. The warm water heats air. This warm, humid air rises. Humid air contains much water. The humid air cools as it rises. It makes clouds. The clouds join together to make thunderstorms. Wind blows the thunderstorms in a circle.

A storm becomes a hurricane when its winds reach 74 miles (119 km) an hour. A hurricane's winds and its thunderstorms do not enter the eye. The eye is the center of the hurricane.

A thick ring of clouds called the eye wall surrounds the eye. The eye wall is the strongest part of a hurricane. Winds blow faster there. Heavy rain and strong thunderstorms come from its clouds.

Hurricanes can travel many miles a day. They stay strong as long as they are over warm ocean water. They may last for weeks. But most hurricanes last about 10 days.

After time, hurricanes become weak and turn into tropical storms. The storms still can cause many problems.

Surges and Tornadoes

In the early 1900s, most hurricane death and damage came from storm surges. A storm surge is made up of huge, heavy waves. Winds from hurricanes push storm surges over land. Storm surges can wash away buildings. People can drown.

Thunderstorms that make up a hurricane may start tornadoes. Tornadoes are spinning winds that blow up to 300 miles (483 km) an hour. Tornadoes can suck up or smash almost everything in their paths. Tornadoes that start over the ocean suck up water. These tornadoes are called waterspouts.

◄ **Many tornadoes start in hurricanes.**

▼ HURRICANES IN HISTORY

Hurricanes are such powerful storms that they have changed history. A hurricane changed history in A.D. 1281. At that time, Mongol ruler Kublai Khan sent 1,000 warships full of soldiers to take over Japan. Japanese samurai soldiers fought the Mongols for seven weeks. Many samurai died. They feared the Mongols soon would win the war.

Then a hurricane blew in from the ocean. Its strong winds and rain sank most of the Mongol ships. More than 100,000 Mongol soldiers died.

Japanese people thanked their storm gods for the kamikaze. Kamikaze means divine wind from the gods.

Hurricanes are powerful storms that can change history. This hurricane is causing coastal floods.

13

Storm Myths

Early people did not understand hurricanes. They told stories called myths to explain how hurricanes worked.

In the stories, gods and goddesses controlled the weather. People believed these gods and goddesses sent hurricanes when people did bad things.

• **In the Antilles,** the Carib Indians believed an evil god called Hurakan started storms. The name hurricane comes from this god's name.

• **In what is now Taiwan,** people believed in the wind-god Hung Kong. They thought Hung Kong sent hurricanes from the China Sea. Hung Kong looked like a giant bird. The people said he flapped his wings to make hurricane winds.

SAFFIR-SIMPSON SCALE

Scientists give each hurricane a number from the Saffir-Simpson Scale. This scale rates a hurricane based on how fast its wind blows. Hurricanes with faster winds cause greater damage than those with weak winds.

	Winds	Storm Surge	Harm
Category 1	74 to 95 miles (119 to 153 km) an hour	4 to 5 feet (1 to 1.5 m) high	Little harm
Category 2	96 to 110 miles (154 to 177 km) an hour	6 to 8 feet (2 to 2.5 m) high	Medium harm to tree branches and street and store signs
Category 3	111 to 130 miles (179 to 209 km) an hour	9 to 12 feet (3 to 3.5 m) high	Heavy harm—parts of trees and roofs damaged
Category 4	131 to 155 miles (211 to 249 km) an hour	13 to 18 feet (4 to 5.5 m) high	Terrible harm to buildings and trees
Category 5	Winds greater than 155 miles (249 km)	Higher than 18 feet (5.5 m)	Buildings and trees blown down

Galveston Hurricane of 1900

On September 8, 1900, a hurricane hit Galveston, Texas. A 20-foot (6-m) high storm surge washed through the town. It smashed most of the town's buildings.

Nuns were in charge of an orphanage. Orphanages are homes for children without parents. The nuns used ropes to tie themselves to rows of children. The nuns wanted to save all the children when the floods came. But the floodwater was too strong and fast. People found the nuns still tied to the children after the flood. They had all drowned.

The storm was the deadliest hurricane in U.S. history. More than 8,000 people died. Bodies floated in the water. They hung in the trees where the waves had swept them. People miles away from Galveston could smell rotting bodies.

A storm surge like this one destroyed Galveston.

EVACUATION
ROUTE

Hurricanes Today

Today, scientists are learning a great deal about hurricanes. But science still has no way to stop hurricanes. Hurricanes can kill people and harm property.

In the early 1960s, the U.S. government started the National Hurricane Center in Miami, Florida. This center is still is use today. Scientists at the center teach people how to protect themselves from hurricanes. Scientists warn people about approaching hurricanes. People then have time to evacuate. Evacuate means to leave quickly.

Signs show people where to go during a hurricane evacuation.

Hurricane Andrew

In 1992, the National Hurricane Center warned people about a strong hurricane named Andrew. Andrew was heading for Florida and Louisiana. More than 1 million people evacuated the areas.

On August 24, 1992, Hurricane Andrew slammed into southern Florida and Louisiana. Heavy rain and a storm surge caused flooding.

Hurricane winds blew down the trees and many cages at the Miami Zoo. But most of the animals lived through the storm. The hurricane also damaged the National Hurricane Center's building and equipment.

Hurricane Andrew destroyed thousands of buildings and left many people homeless. It killed 23 people. Its damage cost more than any hurricane in U.S. history. Scientists retired Hurricane Andrew's name.

Hurricane Andrew blew down trees and overturned cars.

Hurricane Mitch

Mitch was the worst hurricane of 1998. This Category-5 hurricane started near Jamaica in the Caribbean Sea. Its winds blew more than 180 miles (290 km) an hour.

Hurricane Mitch smashed into Honduras and Nicaragua. It dumped up to 70 inches (178 cm) of rain. This caused major flooding and landslides. Water and mud destroyed roads and buildings. Entire neighborhoods slid down steep mountainsides. The storm blew down power lines. Most people in these countries had no electricity or running water.

Hurricane Mitch caused billions of dollars in property loss. It killed more than 12,000 people. It left more than 3 million people without homes.

Hurricane Floyd

In 1999, Hurricane Floyd struck the United States. It weakened when it came over land and became a tropical storm. It brought heavy rains to North Carolina. The rains started floods. North Carolina had the worst flooding in its history. Floods caused millions of dollars in damage.

 Scientists retired Hurricane Mitch's name because it was such a damaging hurricane.

▼ Hurricanes and Science

The National Hurricane Center learned from the problems it faced during Hurricane Andrew. The U.S. government built a new place to house the center. The new building is strong enough to stand through Category-3 winds and floods.

Better Tools

The National Hurricane Center uses new Doppler radar to help track hurricanes. Doppler radar is a machine that measures wind and rain.

Satellites are spacecraft sent into space. Satellites take pictures of clouds. They record wind speed. They send this information to Earth for scientists to study.

◀ **Satellites take pictures of hurricanes. This is what a hurricane looks like from space.**

Hurricane Hunters

Flying inside hurricanes is the best way to learn about them. Trained pilots and scientists fly airplanes into hurricanes. These people are called hurricane hunters.

Hurricane hunters fly airplanes that have radar on them. Radar tells scientists about wind speed and rainfall amounts in different parts of hurricanes. Hurricane hunters drop probes into hurricanes. Probes are machines with computers inside them. As probes fall, they record wind speeds in different parts of the storms. Probes send information back to the airplane.

Watches, Warnings, and Evacuations

Scientists do not know where and when a hurricane will hit until it is close to land. But they now can give people warning when hurricanes are about to strike.

Scientists give a hurricane watch if a hurricane may reach land within 36 hours. People in the path of the hurricane should watch the weather. They should listen to radio and television news to learn more.

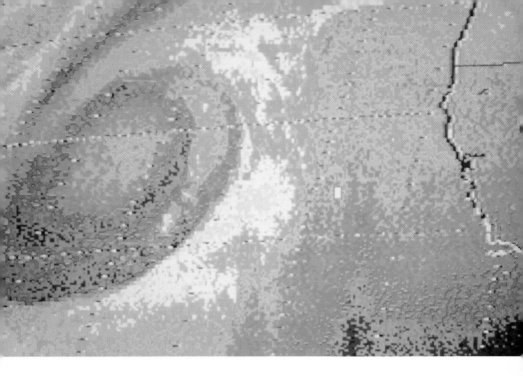

▲ Radar tells scientists where hurricanes are. Red areas show where heavy rain is falling.

The National Hurricane Center gives a warning when a hurricane will reach land in 24 hours or less. The government may order people to evacuate places the hurricane will hit. People must leave when they are told to evacuate.

People can protect their property from hurricanes before they evacuate. People can cover their windows with boards. They can tie down anything that might blow away. Stacking bags of sand around houses helps block out floodwaters.

Hurricanes in the Future

People in the past have thought of many ways to stop hurricanes. Some scientists believed bombing hurricanes would stop them. They hoped the bombs would slow down the winds. Other scientists wanted to cool the oceans by floating large chunks of ice in them. Scientists have proved these ideas will not work. No one knows how to stop hurricanes.

Some scientists fear that the future will bring more hurricanes than ever. These scientists believe Earth is getting warmer. They fear hotter weather will make ocean water warmer. Warmer water could cause more and stronger hurricanes.

Each year, scientists learn more about hurricanes. They want to track hurricanes better. By doing this, they hope to save lives.

No one knows how to stop hurricanes from flooding land. Hurricane Floyd caused this flooding in North Carolina.

GLOSSARY

equator (i-KWAY-tur)—an imaginary line around the center of Earth; the equator divides Earth into two equal halves.

evacuate (i-VAK-yoo-ayt)—to leave quickly

eye (EYE)—the center of a hurricane; a hurricane's eye is calm and clear.

eye wall (EYE WAHL)—a ring of thick clouds that surrounds a hurricane's eye; the eye wall is the strongest part of the hurricane.

kamikaze (kah-mi-KAH-zee)—Japanese word that means Divine Wind from the gods

retire (ri-TIRE)—to remove from use

satellite (sa-TUH-lite)—equipment sent into space to circle Earth; some satellites record information about Earth.

storm surge (STORM SURGE)—large ocean waves pushed over land by a hurricane's wind

tropical (TRAHP-i-kuhl)—a hot area near the equator

ADDRESSES AND INTERNET SITES

Federal Emergency Management Agency
Federal Center Plaza
500 C Street SW
Washington, DC 20472

National Hurricane Center
11691 SW 17th Street
Miami, FL 33165

FEMA for Kids: The Disaster Area
http://www.fema.gov/kids/dizarea.htm

Hurricane Hunter's Home Page
http://www.hurricanehunters.com

Hurricane: Storm Science
http://falcon.miamisci.org/hurricane/hurricane0.
   html

National Hurricane Center
http://www.nhc.noaa.gov

INDEX